Date: 12/13/21

J PRILEPSKIY
Prilepskiy, Danielle,
Superhero Lilly /

PALM BEACH COUNTY
LIBRARY SYSTEM
3650 SUMMIT BLVD.
WEST PALM BEACH, FL 33406

Superhero Lilly

By Danielle Prilepskiy

© 2021 by Danielle Prilepskiy

All rights reserved

ISBN: 978-1-716-18111-5

Lulu.com

Table of Contents

1 Bad News Come Suddenly............ 4

2 We Need to Do Something............ 8

3 Lilly Decides to Become a Superhero...12

4 Do Not Give Up! 15

5 The Lab Looks Like a Secret Place 18

6 Timmy Got a Phone Call 22

7 The World is Saved!................. 24

1 Bad News Come Suddenly

I was in the backyard with my little brother, Timmy, when I sensed something a little...well, I do not know how to explain it. Out of the ordinary...maybe weird...I am not sure. It was just... different. I never felt anything like this before. I mean, you could already tell me I was different. I could hear, smell, see, touch, and taste more than anyone else. Weird? No. Super, super, super weird?

You got that right. I could hear the dog standing at our back door before he even came. I could feel the closed classroom door in my middle school. I knew what was going on inside. You got the point. Simply saying, I got super-senses. So did my family, but I got the most extreme super-senses. I went beyond.

It was a little overwhelming to me when I could feel everything around. Just imagine! Trust me, sometimes it was great but often it was just plain horrible. Anyway, I went back into the house to get an ice-cold drink from the fridge when I felt something strange in the living room. Something near the TV was wrong. I turned it on right in the minute when the locals announced a new coronavirus as a global crisis for everyone. "Dad, can you come here real quick?" I yelled. "Lilly, is that you? I am having a conference. Can it wait?" he replied from the upstairs. "No, hurry!" I screamed. *Why is my family always the busiest where is something important going on? Seriously?* "Coming. What is it?" asked my dad. I was surprised he barely even cared. "Dad, look at the news. There was a new coronavirus in Wuhan, China, and now it is in the USA!" I pointed to the

TV screen. "Oh, dear, this is a problem. Marie, can you come here for a minute?" he asked. My mom didn't have to be told twice; she scurried to the living room. "What is the dilemma?" she asked in a worried voice. We told her all the details.

2. We Need to Do Something

"Oh, my, how it could happen? Timmy! Timmy, come back into the house, NOW!" she yelled at the top of her lungs. With a coronavirus on the loose, she definitely didn't want a single kid outside. Timmy ran into the house as fast as his little feet could go. He was covered head-to-toe in mud, and it even got all over his khakis and a blue shirt. "What do you want? I was playing soccer in the backyard!" He was startled with her yelling at him for no reason. "Timmy, no need to argue, just do as I say. There is a global crisis..." I never got to finish. In a second Timmy, who was 5, looked at TV. He started to cry. "Timmy, stop crying. Go to your room, please. I will meet you there," my dad told him. "Same with you, Miss Lilly. Up into your bedroom! Watch some videos, you two. We will be fine." He nodded at me.

Later that night, as I finished brushing my teeth, I heard my parents discussing what to buy and where to get it. Then they came to the second floor to give me a huge lecture about how I was supposed to be in my bed, relaxing like Timmy. I went back to bed, but I couldn't help thinking about the virus story. I wished it to be over. I was frustrated, overwhelmed, and maybe even a little scared.

For the next couple of weeks the news became worse and worse, so my parents didn't let Timmy and me to continue watching them. Our schools closed, and we had to go into a quarantine. It was boring, but I had my Superhero comics which was all I needed.

I remember the day when I realized my superpower skills like if I was a Superhero. I remembered what happened a few years ago when I went skiing. I got some random senses of everyone and everything around that ski hill. It was great! Wait a second. You are not a superHERO. You have not done anything heroic, yet. I guess you are just SuperLilly, without the Hero part. I wondered about that for at least 15 minutes, thinking if I would ever be worthy enough to consider myself a hero. All important in life I did was my help to Timmy when he was trying to walk with his broken ankle around the house last year. That's all. It is definitely not heroic. I decided to keep thinking of how to become a hero when Timmy came to my room. "Hey," he proclaimed. "Hey," I replied. "What's up?" "Nothing." "Are you bored? I, sure, am." "I am not." I lied. Am I really not bored? Like really, Lilly. "Hey, you know what would be cool?" Timmy whispered. "What?" I replied half-bored, half-annoyed that he still was in my room. "If someone could make a cure for the virus. Vaccine or something... Like if someone could figure out how to end this problem. I bet that person would become a hero of the entire world for sure." A hero to the entire world? Woah, that would be huge! I do not even know anyone besides my neighbors. The whole world...

3 Lilly Decides to Become a Superhero

"Timmy! You got it!! Thank you so much!" I excitedly announced. "Huh? Got what? All I got is a boring summer!" Timmy replied with his face full of gloom. I quickly explained the scenario to Timmy. "You see, brother, I would be a superHero to solve the global crisis." "Woah, that is smart! You will need my help for sure!" Timmy was not bored anymore. Instead, he looked very happy while saying that.

That night we started on our new mission: MISSION TO STOP THE VIRUS! We tried brainstorming ideas, but only simple and useless plans came up to our heads. *I do not know how we are going to have a chance since we can't even get out from our house. I wish I had a superpower to see beyond the house without actually getting out of it...* "Wait a second, I do have a superpower!" I exclaimed, "So do you, Timmy!"

That night was the best night ever. Timmy and I practiced to see far away. After all we could do it. I looked 100 miles out of our house, and I was able to see the barn in Springville, Colorado. "Sis, that's far! You are so good!" my brother told me. "Hey, thanks. You are good too!" I replied. Yes, he was, but not as fortunate as me.

He could only see 2 miles from here. Timmy has to basically strain his whole body for it. We decided to meet in my room every day near 11 am to practice more. The idea was to reach 6000 miles away goal, eventually. That distance should be enough to 'land' us right in Wuhan, China. Yes, it is impossible, but that's what we planned to do.

4 Do not Give Up!

After 10 weeks, Timmy and I were a little happy about our progress, but not really. I could see 2000 miles away, and Timmy could see 50. "C'mon, we are never going to get to 6000! It's impossible," Timmy said. He was exasperated and defeated. "Tiny Tim, when do you ever give up? Certainly, not now. We can do it, I believe it," I replied. However, in my mind I still was not sure. *Maybe this was a bad idea after all. Maybe I can't. Maybe Timmy can't. Maybe it's over. I can't. I will. If… Maybe I can, maybe I can't, maybe I will.*

I did not know what to expect. Nothing was getting better, and I did not know if it was possible. What if I am just wasting my time? Finally, I decided not to give up, and Timmy agreed with me. After what felt like a million hours, a thousand days, and a hundred weeks, I got to the desired 6000 miles. "Yes! Yes! YES!" Timmy exclaimed! "Shh, quiet down. Remember, we did not want Mam and Dad to hear any of this," I whispered. "Oh, yea, my bad," he stated. "Sorry," he looked at me. "Now what?"

I told him that we need to investigate the lab. I was not sure yet, but there was my intuition that we are going to the right direction. I predicted that some dangerous biological experiments may be involved. "Really? You are taking it too seriously, Lilly." "I am not! Did you forget that I am the one who is seeing, and you are the one who is listening?"

I used my senses, and I was 'going' around Wuhan, China (It seemed like I was exploring on Google Maps). I saw a lot of abandoned houses. I bet I am in the right spot! Wow! Suddenly I noticed a little sign "Beware, There are Dangers that Scare." What can it be? I mean, what is the worst that can happen? Timmy was trying to look inside the creepy looking building with no windows (sort of a hut, actually). but he couldn't. Google Maps had a dead end there, and that was it.

5 The Lab Looks Like a Secret Place

I walked (or looked) my mind into it, and what I saw was a lab. I wonder why there's a creepy lab in a deserted neighborhood in Wuhan, China. Then I noticed all of those biological weapons looking right into my eye. I was familiar with them while searching for the information about biological means that could be the cause of the coronavirus.

Anyway, I was sure I found the right place. People in lab coats and strange spiky hair all around their heads were very busy. They seemed jotting down something on a crumpled piece of paper. My mind, being the dumb brain it is, decided to go and take a look.

I noticed a note with a few words. Meet me at 10:00. I've found it! It was 9:50 when I "left" my room, and I was here for about 5 minutes at most. I waited 5 more minutes, and just like I expected, an old man with a beard entered the room. His lab coat was long and wrinkled. "I found the cure. Now we can send a letter to those brainwashed scientists to find it. If all goes well, we will be able to throw them off and give them the wrong one, making them think they got the correct one", he whispered. "Oh yes, and if they realize what happened, we will prove that we have the actual cure with ease", the other man replied.

I knew what to do. I had to call the CDC. When I did, I heard an unknown voice that sounded artificial, like a robotic voice. I was not sure if I am talking to an actual person or just an answer machine. "Um, hi! My name is Lilly Saviok. My brother and I just found a cure to the coronavirus", I whispered. *I couldn't believe I just said that.* Timmy was sitting on my bed, quiet as a mouse. He wanted to hear the news I was about to tell them. "Hello? May I ask who are you? the voice asked. "Um, hi, I mean hello, my name is Lilly, and my brother and I just found a cure to the coronavirus", I repeated. "I know this is not relevant, but I am wondering how old are you? Your voice does not sound very adult-like." "Oh, I am not an adult. I am 10, and my brother is 5," I told the voice. "Excuse me? Where are your parents? A cure to the coronavirus? 10 and 5? This must be a joke? Sorry, I have better things to do. As you may know, we are handling a global crisis." Timmy rolled his eyes in annoyance. "Sorry, Mr. or Mrs., yes, I am a kid and so is my brother, but do not count us out. I promise you, we did find the cure. Well, actually, we know where it is located. We just need your help," I explained.

10 minutes later my conversation with the voice, who turned to be a real man, ended. At first, he was flabbergasted, but then he realized that I may be right. He put me on hold to talk to his co-workers who happened to be some army people. Then he mentioned the plan to go to Wuhan, China for visiting the lab. It could take some time to find out what is going on there, so I knew that I was in to the wait.

6 Timmy Got a Phone Call

Timmy received a phone call 2 weeks later. The same man said that they broke into the secret lab. They found some scientists there and, most importantly, the proper cure. Volunteers tried if it was the actual cure, and it worked. Is not it wonderful?!

Like my mom says when she wants to lecture us about how we shouldn't get revenge on people, "What goes around, comes around!". Those lab scientists confessed that they were trying to help out their faraway unknown island by getting themselves to be the richest people on the planet. Why? To make the other countries have to pay thousands, MILLIONS dollars to get a tiny dose of the cure medication. Those scientists specifically decided to build some random hut in the middle of Wuhan, China so people would suspect anyone but them. They tried, but their revenge on everyone else got right back to them like a boomerang.

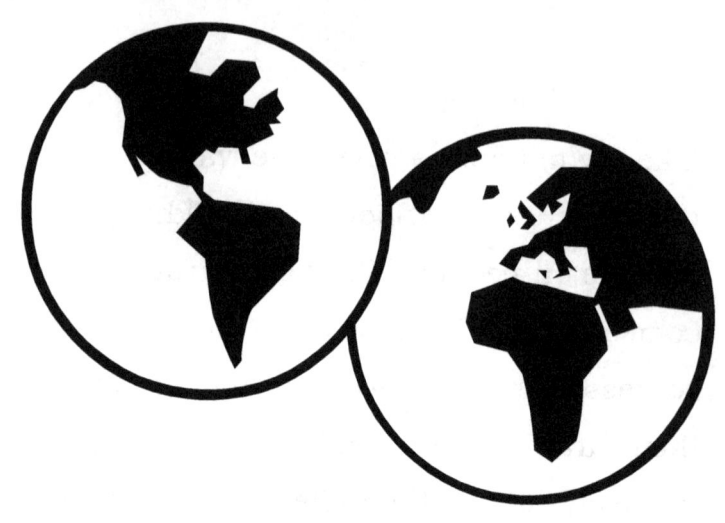

7 The World is Saved!

In the beginning of July the quarantine was over. Everyone was happy to go back to the normal lifestyle. People could do what they wanted without worries. It was great! Stockholm, Sweden supposed to be live-streamed on July 2nd which would be when...wait for it...wait for it...My brother and I would get the Nobel Prize! The only problem was that we had to go on a plane to Stockholm, but whatever.

I can't believe I even mentioned that. It was astonishing, amazing, and unbelievable! I obviously got to have the pleasure of telling my parents about the whole thing. "We are so happy for you, Lilly! You too, Tiny Tim. You guys did great!" my dad exclaimed. "C'mon, what are we waiting for? Let's go to get some cake and celebrate!" my mom excitedly told us in a rush.

The next day was the live stream, and I stood on the stage so proudly with my younger brother, smiling for the cameras. It was a delight! My parents were beaming with joy, and the whole audience was so relieved for the vaccine. "Hey, Lilly?" Timmy whispered into my ear. "Yeah, Timmy?" I answered back. "I shouldn't be standing here right now. It was all you. You solved that mystery, not me."

I smiled, "Thanks, Timmy. To be honest, I have to say I couldn't have done it without you. I am serious." His smile glimmered and shined, and he was as happy as could be.

All those days were extraordinary ones for certain. My mind was so focused on my accomplishment, that I didn't have time for anything else. *You are not SuperLilly anymore. You are a hero. You are Superhero Lilly, with the "hero" part, for sure!*

About the Author

Danielle Prilepskiy lives in Cleveland, Ohio. She likes playing tennis, listening to music, and writing books.

You might also like **Sam Plays Detective** by Danielle Prilepskiy.

CPSIA information can be obtained
at www.ICGtesting.com
Printed in the USA
LVHW080920251121
704424LV00002B/151